Our Puppy's Holiday

For John, Martina, Sophie and Gemma Aston –
and Paddy

Our Puppy's Holiday

Ruth Brown

Beaver Books

F

A Beaver Book
Published by Arrow Books Limited
62-65 Chandos Place, London WC2N 4NW
An imprint of Century Hutchinson Ltd

London Melbourne Sydney Auckland
Johannesburg and agencies throughout the world

First published by Andersen Press 1987

Beaver edition 1988

© Ruth Brown 1987

Printed and bound in Italy by Grafiche AZ, Verona

ISBN 0 09 954800 3

It was our puppy's first holiday.

**Everything was new to her:
the wide, wide beach,**

the screeching gulls

and the crashing waves.

She played hide-and-seek

and follow my leader

and leap-frog

and another game of hide-and-seek,

this time with a difference!

There were new things to eat

and drink!

There were hills to climb

and walls to climb.

But an old tree was a problem

in more ways than one.

She made friends – sometimes easily

sometimes not so easily.

She was having such a good time

that she just wanted to go on playing

and playing

even in the dark!

For she didn't know – that it was only the first day!

Other titles in the Beaver/Sparrow Picture Book series:

An American Tail

The Bad Babies Counting Book Tony Bradman and Debbie
   van der Beek

Bear Goes to Town Anthony Browne

The Big Sneeze Ruth Brown

Crazy Charlie Ruth Brown

The Grizzly Revenge Ruth Brown

If At First You Do Not See Ruth Brown

Our Cat Flossie Ruth Brown

Harriet and William and the Terrible Creature Valerie Carey
   and Lynne Cherry

In the Attic Hiawyn Oram and Satoshi Kitamura

Ned and the Joybaloo Hiawyn Oram and Satoshi Kitamura

What's Inside? Satoshi Kitamura

The Adventures of King Rollo David McKee

The Further Adventures of King Rollo David McKee

The Hill and the Rock David McKee

I Hate My Teddy Bear David McKee

King Rollo's Letter and Other Stories David McKee

King Rollo's Playroom David McKee

Not Now Bernard David McKee

Two Can Toucan David McKee

Two Monsters David McKee

Tusk Tusk David McKee

The Truffle Hunter Inga Moore

The Vegetable Thieves Inga Moore

Babylon Jill Paton Walsh and Jennifer Northway

Robbery at Foxwood Cynthia and Brian Paterson

The Foxwood Treasure Cynthia and Brian Paterson

The Foxwood Regatta Cynthia and Brian Paterson

The Foxwood Kidnap Cynthia and Brian Paterson

The Tiger Who Lost His Stripes Anthony Paul and
   Michael Foreman

The Magic Pasta Pot Tomie de Paola

Mary Had a Little Lamb Tomie de Paola

We Can Say No! David Pithers and Sarah Greene

The Boy Who Cried Wolf Tony Ross

Goldilocks and the Three Bears Tony Ross

The Three Pigs Tony Ross

Terrible Tuesday Hazel Townson and Tony Ross

There's A Crocodile Under My Bed Dieter and Ingrid Schubert

Emergency Mouse Bernard Stone and Ralph Steadman

Inspector Mouse Bernard Stone and Ralph Steadman

Quasimodo Mouse Bernard Stone and Ralph Steadman

The Fox and the Cat Kevin Crossley-Holland and Susan Varley

Crocodile Teeth Marjorie Ann Watts

The Tale of Fearsome Fritz Jeanne Willis and Margaret Chamberlain

The Tale of Mucky Mabel Jeanne Willis and Margaret Chamberlain